Bedtime Stories
for kids

Uncle Amon

Published by Hey Sup Bye Publishing

ISBN-13: 978-1515376842
ISBN-10: 1515376842

TABLE OF CONTENTS

Little Star Friends

"Good night Charlie," said Mother, giving her six year old son a kiss on his cheek.

"Aren't you going to read me a bedtime story?" asked Charlie.

"Oh yes," said Mother, picking a book off Charlie's bookshelf. "Of course I am."

Mother started reading Charlie a bedtime story about the stars in the sky and soon he was fast asleep. Charlie had images of stars in his mind when he fell asleep. He started dreaming about what it would be like to live in the stars.

"It would be fun going from one star to another," said Charlie to himself in his dream. "I could live on a different star each night."

Charlie dreamt about how he could move around the universe sleeping on whatever star he felt like. In his dream he met up with some very friendly little star friends. They liked Charlie immediately and followed him wherever he went. They glowed a special light on him just to keep him safe.

"Thank you my star friends," said Charlie. "I feel very safe out here with you."

The star friends showed Charlie some of the brightest stars in the universe.

"Wow!" exclaimed Charlie. "These stars are very bright!"

The star friends gave Charlie a pair of sunglasses to shield his eyes from the bright light.

"That is better," said Charlie, putting the sunglasses on.

The little star friends showed Charlie some of the coldest stars in the universe. These were stars that were right on the very edge of the universe.

"Oh my!" exclaimed Charlie. "These stars are cold."

The little star friends gave Charlie a warm sweater and pair of mittens to put on so that he could stay warm.

"Thank you," said Charlie, appreciating the warm clothing.

"Charlie!" exclaimed a familiar voice, shaking him. "It is time to wake up!"

Charlie opened his eyes and saw his Mother trying to wake him up. He was back in his room and the stars and his little star friends were gone.

"Where are all my new little star friends?" asked Charlie.

"I don't know what you are talking about," said Mother. "And what are you doing with sunglasses, a sweater and mittens on."

Charlie looked down and he laughed as he noticed that he had on a pair of sunglasses, a sweater and a pair of mittens.

"My new little star friends gave me these," said Charlie. "So that I could stay warm on the stars."

"I see," said Mother. "Well let's get you dressed. We have a busy day ahead of us."

"Yes Mother," said Charlie.

There were several other times that Charlie's little star friends came to him in his dreams. His little star friends took him on many star adventures. Charlie enjoyed his time in the stars and his new little star friends very much.

Pirate Ship Adventure

Sammy was a six year old little boy who lived in an imaginary world with his imaginary friends. One day, Sammy was pondering what he wanted to do for an adventure. He decided that he wanted to go on an adventure on a pirate ship and he wanted to find some buried treasure.

"Oh yes," dreamed Sammy. "An adventure on a pirate ship would be just the adventure I need."

Sammy thought long and hard about the new adventure he wanted to go on. He thought about how much fun it would be to actually meet up with some pirates. However, then he started to think about the danger he could face with the pirates and he was a little reluctant to go on a pirate ship adventure.

Sammy found his best friend, Stephen, sitting outside on a big rock.

"Stephen," said Sammy. "I was thinking of going on an adventure on a pirate ship."

"Oh now that would be some adventure," said Stephen. "Being on the high seas, rocking back and forth in the waves. However, do you know how dangerous that adventure would be?"

"Yes," said Sammy. "That is why I am thinking twice about going on it."

"I see," said Stephen. "That is probably a smart move. However, what if you were to board the pirate ship without the pirates seeing you? If you did that you wouldn't have to fear the pirates because they wouldn't know you were there."

"Now," said Sammy. "That is a plan. Okay, I am going on an adventure on a pirate ship."

Sammy walked down to the ocean front and he saw a pirate ship sitting in the bay. The ship was dirty looking and very dark but that did not deter him.

Sammy waited until all of the pirates had gotten off the pirate ship and then he quickly boarded it. He found an old wooden crate at the far end of the ship and he hid behind it.

A few hours later, Sammy saw that the pirates were returning to the ship and in minutes of their return, he felt the ocean waves building up around him on both sides. He felt the ship moving further into the deep waters of the ocean.

Once they had gotten quite a ways out into the ocean waters, Sammy overheard a conversation between the pirates about a treasure chest that they were going to find.

"It is located on that little island we visited last week," said the one pirate.

"Where on the island?" asked the other.

"Underneath the tallest tree on the island," said the first pirate.

Once the pirates had landed the ship on the island, Sammy waited until the coast was clear and then he stepped down off the ship and onto the island. Sammy looked all around the island and he saw the tallest tree on the other end of the beach where he was standing. He made his way over to it.

He looked underneath the tree and he had found the treasure chest. He was so excited that he wanted to shout but he knew the pirates would find him if he did.

Sammy lifted the lid on the treasure chest and he saw jewels and coins glitter in the sunlight. He was just going to pick up one of the jewels when he saw pirates coming straight toward him.

Sammy ran in the opposite direction as quickly as he could. He didn't want the pirates to chase him. He found a cave and he hid there. He watched as the pirates lifted the treasure chest and carried it toward their ship. Sammy was relieved that they hadn't caught him.

After the pirates had left, he turned around inside the cave he was in and he saw treasure chest after treasure chest lined up against the far wall of the cave.

"I am so rich!" explained Sammy happily.

Sammy built himself a raft and he drifted home. He told Stephen about the treasure and they both decided they were going to go back to the island and bring the treasure chests home so they could share the treasure with their family and friends.

"Thank you for sharing the treasure with me!" exclaimed Sammy's Mother when he gave her a treasure chest all for herself.

Sammy and Stephen's family and friends were very happy and they decided they would make a special holiday in Sammy and Stephen's honor.

Adventure to the Moon

"I am bored," said Andrew, a five year old boy. "I want to go on an adventure."

Andrew looked around his room and he saw a picture book of the solar system on his desk. That gave him an idea.

"I want to go on an adventure to the moon," said Andrew. "I want to be an astronaut."

Andrew thought about how he could be an astronaut and he wasn't sure how he could do it.

"The moon is so far away," said Andrew to himself. "How will I ever be able to get to it?"

"You can build a rocket ship," said Andrew's best friend, Peter.

"Yes," said Andrew. "A rocket ship! That is how I will get to the moon.

Andrew and Peter built a rocket ship out of a cardboard box. They covered the outside of it with tin foil.

"Are you ready to go to the moon now?" asked Peter, when the rocket ship was finished.

"Yes," said Andrew. "I am ready to go to the moon."

Peter started the countdown.

"Ten, nine, eight," said Peter.

Andrew and the cardboard rocket ship flew off into space. They flew past the tall buildings and the tall trees. They flew past the clouds and then they flew through the atmosphere.

"Oh look at all the pretty stars in the sky," said Andrew to himself.

Andrew liked flying around in space. It was very quiet there. Andrew had a lot of time to look out the window of his rocket ship. Pretty soon a big round object came into view.

"There is the moon!" exclaimed Andrew.

Andrew was so excited to see the moon that he forgot to land on it.

"Oh dear," said Andrew. "I forgot to land on the moon. I guess I will have to orbit it and then land."

Andrew steered the rocket ship around the moon and this time when he saw the landing site, he carefully landed his rocket ship on the surface.

"Oh my!" exclaimed Andrew, getting out of the rocket ship and walking around the surface of the moon. "It sure is lonely looking here. I think I will go and explore it some more."

Andrew took his space vehicle out of his rocket ship and he drove around the surface of the moon.

"All I see is dust and craters," said Andrew.

Andrew put the space vehicle into the rocket ship and he headed back home. He enjoyed seeing the green grass and the green leaves on the trees. He had a whole new appreciation for the things that were on Earth.

"You wouldn't believe how dusty and lonely the moon was," said Andrew, when he arrived back home.

"Are you saying you didn't have a good time?" asked Peter.

"Oh no!" exclaimed Andrew. "Actually, it was quite the opposite."

"Would you go to the moon again?" asked Peter.

"Yes," said Andrew, without hesitation. "I definitely would!"

The Magical Frog

Lilly, a young girl of seven years old, was sitting on a park bench, reading her favorite book. She was getting sleepy so she laid her sweater on the bench and laid down on top of it.

"Lilly," someone called to her while she was sleeping. "Wake up."

Lilly woke up from her sleep and she saw a frog sitting on the very edge of the park bench. The frog was talking to her. She couldn't believe it so she rubbed eyes and opened them again. It didn't make a difference though, the frog was still there and he was still talking to her.

"Why are you talking to me?" asked Lilly. "Frogs aren't supposed to be able to talk."

"Well," said the frog. "I can talk because I am magical."

"I don't believe you," said Lilly. "Prove to me that you are magical."

"Okay," said the frog. "Do you see that nice big stone over there on the walkway?"

"Yes," said Lilly. "I do."

"Good," said the frog. "Please go pick it up."

"Okay," said Lilly.

Lilly picked up the stone and she held it in her hand.

"Do you feel something different about that stone?" asked the frog.

"Well," said Lilly. "Yes, I actually do. It is warm."

"Good," said the frog. "Now, hold out your and toward me and put the stone in the center of your palm."

Lilly did as she was told.

"Hocus pocus!" exclaimed the frog. "Hocus pocus! Please turn this stone into a gem right in front of our eyes."

Lilly couldn't believe it, but there in her hand was the most beautiful gem that she had ever seen. It was a bright blue color and it gleamed radiantly in the sunlight.

"I can't believe this," said Lilly. "You really are magical."

Lilly sat in amazement, staring at the beautiful gem in her hand.

"It is beautiful," said Lilly.

"So, do you like the gem?" asked the frog.

"Yes," said Lilly. "Yes, yes I do!"

"It is magical," said the frog.

"What do you mean?" asked Lilly.

"Make a wish," said the frog.

"I wish for an ice cream cone," said Lilly.

In an instant a large ice cream cone was in Lilly's hand.

"Oh my!" exclaimed Lilly, licking the ice cream cone.

"You must use this gem for good only," said the frog.

"Thank you," said Lilly.

Lilly took the gem and finished her ice cream cone. She fell back to sleep on the park bench.

"Wake up Lilly," a familiar voice said.

Lilly woke up and she saw her mother standing over her. She looked down at her hand. The gem was still there.

"My!" exclaimed Mother. "What a beautiful gem you have? Where did you get it from?"

"I got it from a magical frog," said Lilly.

Lilly took her gem home with her and every day she used it to wish for something good to happen and every day something good did happen.

"Can I see your magical gem?" asked her older brother, Theodore, one day.

"I guess," said Lilly. "Why do you want to see it?"

"I want to wish that I don't have to go to school tomorrow," said Theodore.

"You can't," said Lilly.

Theodore grabbed the gem and hid it behind his back.

"Hocus pocus," laughed Theodore. "I wish that I don't have to go to school tomorrow."

All of a sudden the gem disintegrated into dust.

"My beautiful gem!" cried Lilly. "What have you done?"

Mother came into Lilly's room to find out what the commotion was.

"Theodore used my gem for something bad," said Lilly.

"Oh dear!" exclaimed Mother, cleaning up the dust from the gem.

"I wish I had my gem back," said Lilly. "I would keep it away from Theodore if I did."

All of a sudden the dust on the dust pan turned back into Lilly's precious gem. She hid the gem under her mattress and would only play with it when Theodore wasn't around.

Where is Teddy?

Four year old Becky was in her room playing with her toys. She had all her dolls and teddy bears laid out on her bed. They were all having a nap after a very busy day they just had.

"It is time to wake up dollies," said Becky, a few minutes later.

Becky woke all her dollies up and dressed them in their most beautiful gowns and silver slippers.

"You are all princesses," said Becky.

Becky looked around for her favorite teddy bear.

"Oh dear," said Becky. "Where is Teddy?"

She looked everywhere for him but she couldn't find him.

"I can't have lost Teddy," said Becky in despair. "He has to be here!"

Becky flung all her dollies onto the floor and took all her blankets off the bed. She looked under her pillow and he wasn't there.

"Oh dear!" cried Becky. "I have lost Teddy!"

Mother came up to the top of the stairs to find out what all the commotion was all about.

"I lost Teddy!" cried Becky.

"Oh dear!" exclaimed Mother. "He has to be here somewhere."

Becky and Mother searched the house upside down and Teddy was nowhere to be found.

"What are you two looking for?" asked Daddy, coming inside from the garage.

"We are looking for Teddy," said Becky. "I lost him."

"I think I saw him in the garage just now," said Daddy.

"What would Teddy be doing in the garage?" asked Becky, while she ran to the garage to go get him.

Becky looked around the garage and she saw a box on the garage floor. She saw Teddy sitting out halfway out of the box.

"Oh Teddy!" cried Becky, happily. "I am so glad I found you!"

Becky bent over to pick Teddy up out of the box and she noticed something moving in the box. She picked it up too.

"A kitten!" exclaimed Becky. "Oh Teddy! You were protecting this precious little kitten."

Becky gave Teddy a hug and a kiss. She took Teddy and the kitten into the house.

"Look where I found Teddy," said Becky. "Teddy was protecting this little baby kitten!"

"That little baby kitten is yours now," said Daddy, winking at Mommy.

"Oh Daddy!" exclaimed Becky. "I love you!"

Becky took good care of the little kitten. She was very happy that she now had a little kitten of her own to play with.

Just for Fun Activity

There are a lot of different adventures in bedtime stories. What kind of adventure would you like to go on? Write a story and draw pictures of your adventure.

Coloring Book Pages

Games and Puzzles

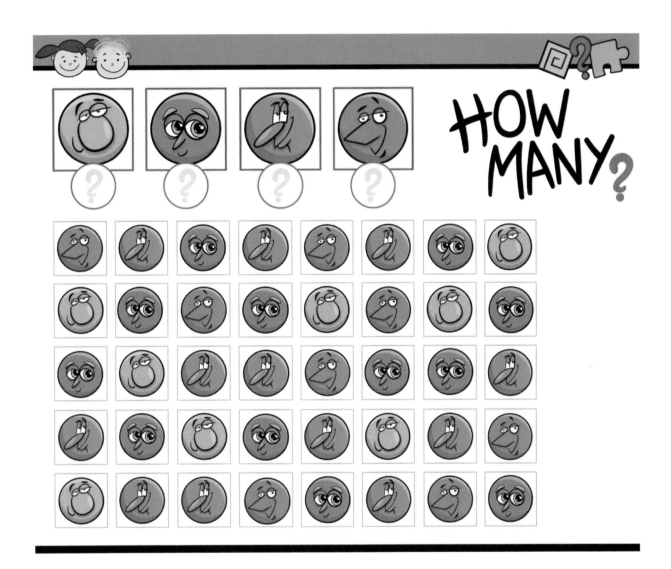

Maze #1

Maze #2

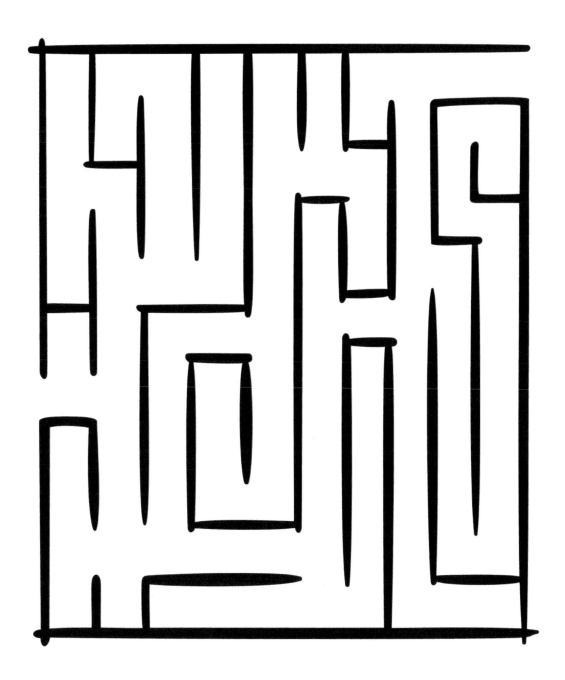

Maze #3

Maze #4

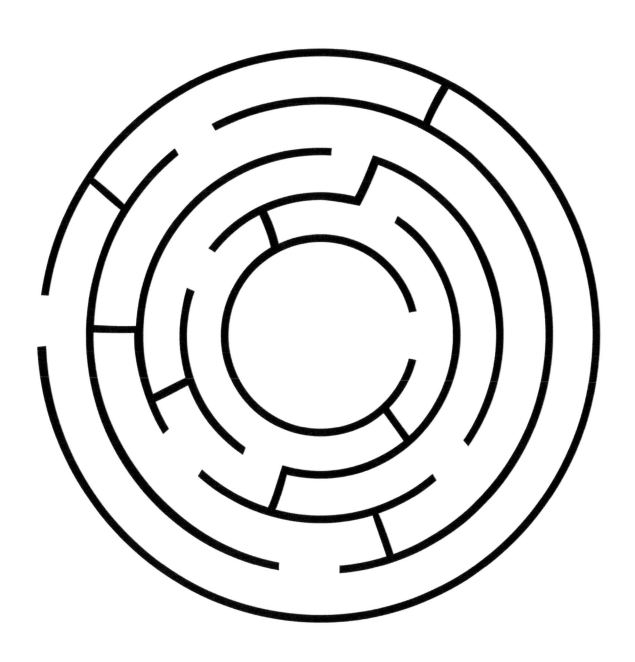

Game and Puzzle Solutions

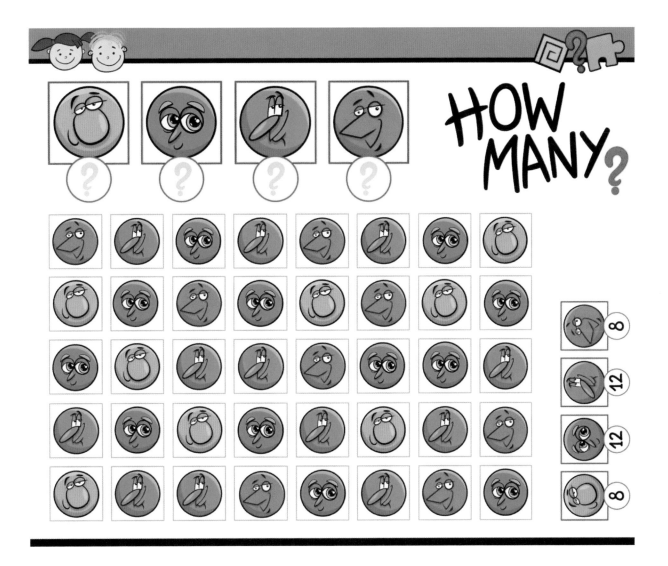

HOW MANY?

About the Author

Uncle Amon began his career with a vision. It was to influence and create a positive change in the world through children's books by sharing fun and inspiring stories. Whether it is an important lesson or just creating laughs, Uncle Amon provides insightful stories that are sure to bring a smile to your face! His unique style and creativity stand out from other children's book authors, because he uses real life experiences to tell a tale of imagination and adventure.

"I always shoot for the moon. And if I miss? I'll land in the stars."
-Uncle Amon

www.uncleamon.com

Printed in Poland
by Amazon Fulfillment
Poland Sp. z o.o., Wrocław